Vain Regrets

A Dream Novel

Vain Regrets

A Dream Novel

DANIEL HILL ZAFREN

Published by Time Treasures Books, Goose Creek, South Carolina
ISBN 13: 978-0-9833042-5-8
Printed in the United States of America

Cover and interior design by Susan Newman Design Inc.

List of earlier memorable works by the author:
In a World We Never Made (2001)
A Door Never Opened (2003)
Shadow Selves (2005)
Network of Death (2006)
Not Lost – Just Not Found (2008)
Restless Beauty (2009)
Glimpses of Forgotten Dreams (2010)
Echo in the Heart (2011)
Double Hugs (2011)
Page Passage (2013)
Wish Winds (2014)
Unfinished Thinking (2015)

Vain Regrets

The sun was setting on a life misspent;
    And as the mind o'er the past years went,
From the dying lips came the sad refrain:
    "Could I but live my life again,
    Oh, then my aim should be so high,
    That at its close I need not cry
    In deep distress, yet all in vain,
    To live the wasted years again!"

— Estelle Mendell

PROLOGUE

He had been there and done that. Most older folks harbor some form of regret concerning events earlier in their lives. Now that Roger Kimbel was in the category as an older folk with regrets, it inspired him to write novels about it with the intention and hope of getting seniors to accept that regrets are in vain and all energy should be concentrated on making the present and future a positive.

Roger started writing after his retirement and had just finished his third novel revolving around this theme. *Glimpses of the Past* was set in a retirement home with a slew of interesting characters demonstrating that seniors have all of their emotions at stake and it is self-defeating to look back over one's shoulder. He theorized in the books and to all who would listen that instead of describing it as a regret, it might be looked at as a turning point. That way it can be considered just a condition that propelled what came next. A mistake is only a regret if nothing is learned from it.

After publication of each book, he would make arrangements for book signings at various senior centers. In addition to any sale of the book, he could possibly initiate personal discussions on the topic. Sales were usually meager, but that was not his primary concern. Few authors can make a living writing and selling the books. Writing for him was a hobby, a hobby with a serious purpose.

The down side of this endeavor was that by broaching the subject in writing and discussion, he was continually reviewing his own past. It became nearly a compulsion to revisit the regrets. Of course, overall his own life was remarkable in the sense that he was happy in old age and that reverberated down to earlier periods. He had never had a serious illness or injury. In fact, he had never had a major operation or even had to stay in a hospital overnight. He had a long and satisfying marriage to a loving wife who proved time and time again to be even-keeled and rationale. After the child-rearing years, she pursued a career of her own.

They had raised two children who never posed a problem. One of life's subtle blessings is to have agreeable children and then grandchildren. He also had a fulfilling professional career over nearly forty years even though it was not what he had hoped to do with his life at an early age. A reasonable person would not file that away as a complaint.

There had been a chain of incidents as a youngster that defied a logical response by him. By all standards they were small stuff, but since he remembered them so vividly after so many years they left a definite scar on his psyche. The first such calamity was in fourth grade when Carol Burns tried to kiss him at school in the coat closet. He cried and ran away. Then there was the time he had broken an expensive antique lamp in the house and lied about blaming his brother for it. His parents believed him so his brother was punished. Naturally, how could he not recall in his naivety at the time when he was a freshman in high school when Georgina Wright invited him to a party at her house, only to discover it was not a party and he was the only one invited and she was scantily dressed in a Japanese silk kimono with nothing on underneath. He ran away as fast as he could, and he was sure that Carol Burns was laughing at him all the way.

The greatest regrets took place when he was in college. He met a sweet and adorable young girl who worshiped him. Regina Stern followed him around just to be close to him. He treated her badly and hurt her deeply. The worst part for him was he actually enjoyed treating her that way, a trait that never reappeared but once in a mean lifetime is enough. One particular upsetting incident he revisited numerous times. It was at a college party. She was there and tried earnestly to talk to him. He just ignored her, even when she pleaded with him. He could still see the hurt in her eyes and the tears flowing down her cheeks. One of his friends castigated him and also said he would give his right arm to have a girl feel that way about him. It did not budge his attention and actions. To this day, he could not believe he had been so callous. At another time, she had given him a thick scrapbook filled with poems she had written to and for him. It must have taken her a long time to create such poetry and put it together in such a nice presentation form. He did not read any of them and just threw the whole thing away. A cold shudder went through him each time he recalled that unnecessarily thoughtless and hurtful act. Years later she became a chronic drug addict and he had harbored guilt that in some way he may have been to blame.

The other incident was that he had befriended several very liberal students who were swept up in an activist role as part of the budding Civil Rights Movement. They wanted him to go with them on a trip to the deep South to help with black voter registration. An earlier group from other schools on a similar quest had disappeared, speculation being that they had been murdered. He was basically scared and would not go. The others went and were beaten and arrested. He always felt he needed to make it up to them somehow, but never did find anything of value or significance to do. He wanted to become an activist leader for all sorts of causes affecting the downtrodden. His best intentions actually produced an inertia. In the deep recesses of his mind and spirit the belief that he could have made a major difference in the world never materialized. It haunted him, and until his writing he was both timid and tentative in matters of pubic events. He shied away from involvement in anything controversial, for which he was not proud.

Obviously, he needed to follow his own advice. As is often the case, it is easier to do for others than it is for oneself. Another regret in vain.

ONE

The world around him was filled with symbols and meanings that he needed to ponder over. It was not just snowing outside; it symbolized the winter of his life. Even the nursing home he was in was a symbol. It represented a final destination on a life that was particularly his own. That life, now that he was able to look back at it, was one big regret from beginning to now. With regret behind and death ahead, it was crucial that the here and now have a special significance.

At eighty years old, Sidney Corwin was examining his existence as he had never done before. In a way, it was the beginning of his life all over again. This amazing transformation was all due to the close friendship that had developed with Roger Kimbel. He had never met an author before, and that was hard to believe for a man of his many years. Roger had said on more than one occasion that there is no such thing as never or always. Even that pronouncement had led Sid to avenues of thought he had not traveled before. After reading all of Roger's books, thoughts were in free flight.

He had met Roger five years earlier when Roger was having a book signing at the senior center attached to the nursing home. At that time, Roger's newest book was *Glimpses of the Past*, a thought-provoking story of some extraordinary folks in a retirement home. It had the often ignored theme that old people are people too. Roger was set up at a small table in the lobby with a stack of the books and brochures before him.

Sid went to the senior center every morning to read the newspaper, an early ritual. A door led directly from the home to the center and was an easy access for those still able to walk. Once through the door, Sid sat on a bench near the door and watched the book signing for awhile. Roger seemed like a pleasant fellow who enjoyed talking to the few folks that stopped by to pick up literature and examine the book. In the time he watched nobody bought a book.

Sid approached the table. He was frail and stooped at the shoulders, an aftermath of the injuries from the accident twenty years earlier. Roger flashed a friendly smile. "Hey there, young fella."

Sid smiled back. The dentures had cost a bundle so he displayed them whenever he could, or more aptly when he remembered to. He knew his voice was weak and hoped he could be heard over the background noise of people talking and music playing. "I think you need to have your glasses checked. I am not sure I was ever a young fella."

Roger chuckled. "Youth is overrated anyway. But, only a young fella would risk seeing what was going on at this table. After all, I am an ole buzzard but like to think I am young in spirit."

Sid was almost serious. "You have to watch out for those spirits. They can gang up on you."

Roger smiled. "Trust me. Spirits are good. Have a seat next to me and we can chat."

Sid had not noticed the empty chair next to Roger and the thought of resting was appealing. He tired easily, and he accepted that as he did all of the adverse things that comprised his life. Roger continued, "Be well and set a spell."

"I will do and sit next to you."

"True. A feisty fellow, aren't you? A man apart and after my own heart."

Between the curiosity seekers, they talked for well over an hour. Sid could not recall a time when he was so engrossed in conversation. Roger filled him in on his background and personal life, and Sid highlighted what he termed a meager and disappointing life. His two big disasters were an empty marriage to an evil woman and the automobile accident nearly twenty years ago that left him incapacitated so he had to live in the home where everything was done for him including housekeeping of his small room and meals brought to him. This minimal existence cost him dearly. The home took all of the small amounts in his savings and checking accounts, all of the settlement funds he received and would receive from the accident except for the price of the dentures and medical expenses, and ninety percent of his monthly social security payments. "I should be a bitter old man, but I don't even have enough feelings to be bitter. I am just passing time until actual death catches up to the nonexistence I suffer through."

"Just from our initial meeting and exchange of words, you don't strike me as the kind of person you describe."

Sid grimaced. "That is probably because you are the first person I have talked to in a long time."

"Things bottled up inside set free?"

"Something like that. Or, maybe it is just grasping at straws."

"Sometimes it doesn't pay to look too closely at things we do."

"Or, don't do."

"Other times it pays to do both. You may not believe this but thinking is a form of feeling."

"You would have to convince me of that."

Roger patted him on the arm. "Do you like to read?"

"Yes."

"I am giving you a copy of my book. Hopefully, you can relate to one or more of the characters and it will revitalize a will to face each day anew. No matter the age or the condition, each of us has the capacity to change who we are and how we look at and accept the world around us. The problem with most people is that they see only what is at the surface. Once you realize it is possible to look beyond that then it becomes easier to live that way as well."

"Are all authors that positive?"

"I don't dare to speak for others, But, it is a basic reality. Each breath we take is new life. So, why can't there also be new insights and new beginnings?"

"Where were you when I needed you, say fifty years ago?"

"It's not too late to make up for lost time."

"I sure wish I could believe that. I better buy the book. It may be a manual for living."

"You don't have to do that. It is a gift, and I am signing it for you."

Sid was speechless. He shook Roger's hand weakly, and totally forgetting about reading the newspaper he headed back to his room clutching the prized possession. He was a man on a mission.

TWO

True to his word, Roger came to visit Sid at the home a week later. Sid could not remember feeling that kind of excited anticipation. They sat on the terrace beneath a large elm tree.

Sid spoke with high animation, another rare personal feature. "I loved *Glimpses of the Past*. I read it three times. The characters are so real. Are they?"

Roger chuckled. "People ask me that often. Except for a few major characters in my books who actually had a significant impact on my life, all my characters are basically from my imagination. They may have hints of me or some other person that may have crossed my path, but characters are really tools to propel the story or to add emphasis to ideas or the philosophy I am trying to convey. Characters are a source for examples and emphasis, or a host of other directions in the literary journey."

Sid was serious when he stammered, "They are more real than I am, and they are examples of the kind of person I should have been."

"I don't think you give yourself enough credit."

"I am looking at myself realistically. If I was a character in your book it would be a blank page. My life is without any achievements."

"I thought we touched on this last week. Whatever you did or did not do, as long as you are alive it is not too late to right a wrong or to live a moment that will be significant."

"Easy for you to say. You have had a successful life capped with the accomplishment of writing books. You have earned the right to brag about who you are and what you have done."

"I dare say, if you look back carefully over all of the years, there are deeds worth relating about because you were successful at them or somebody benefited by them."

"If there were any such miracles, I have long since forgotten them."

"You probably just need a refresher course on looking backward. Then, you can take the course on looking ahead."

Sid looked deep into Roger's eyes as if he were seeking his own image in them. "I must admit your book made me think longer and harder than I have in a long time."

"Proves my point."

"I am not sure any thinking at my age is beneficial. It gives emphasis to my weaknesses and lends new significance to my failures."

"Weakness is a very human quality, and if one is weak in one category it often is offset by a greater strength somewhere else. Failure is a matter of degree and interpretation. It is not an end or an exit. It merely means we have to find a different way to do this or that, and start in another direction. Besides, people are hard on themselves. What may be a failure to you may not appear that way to others."

"I know what I wasn't and what I did not do."

"With no excuses?"

"None to satisfy me."

"You sure like to beat yourself up."

"I deserve it."

"I don't think so. I believe you need to revisit the seasons of your life and look at everything as it was at the time and not in hindsight. I am sure you will conclude that at that time, that place, and under those circumstances you exercised the best course of action. It is a subjective judgment and not an objective one dictating what might have been the right thing to do. I have seen it more than once that there can be a vast difference between what is right and what is best."

"I would like to buy all of your books."

"Are you sure?"

"I am sure. I know I can learn much from you."

"Before I go, I'll get them for you. I carry copies in the trunk of the car as I can't predict when some nice young fella will come along and want to fatten his library with them. I'll give you a special price."

"They don't let me keep much money, but I think I can cover it. If they all have the same enjoyment factor as this one, you have a loyal fan for life, as limited as that might be."

"I already have a President of my fan club. I can make you the Vice President."

"That might be my only achievement."

"It is a start and not an end."

THREE

That was the beginning of the meaningful friendship. Sid also bought each new book as Roger finished it. He read them all multiple times. There was the rich enjoyment of the stories, life lessons that he certainly would have used if he had become what he thought he wanted to do earlier in life, as well as the characters as people he was envious of because of their talents and grasp of living. Then there were the themes and ideas that he digested as if he were thinking of them himself and closely involved in their evolution and resolution.

A concept in a few of the books that peaked his attention was that of a turning point in life. A turning point is an event, a notion, or a person that affects the direction of one's life. He spent long hours revisiting episodes in his life that impacted what he did, why he did it, and what the consequences were or might have been.

He had also talked about that kind of exploration with Roger numerous times over the years. Both men concluded that for some there was only one major turning point; for others there could be more than one. There might also be one or a series of minor turning points.

Sid was sure there was only one turning point in his life and it was early. It was when he went to college. As an only child from a middle class family it was a given that he would go to college. His parents had saved for that event. The problem was what to study and where to go. Sid had been a mediocre student in high school with a void in extracurricular activities. He was also socially withdrawn and deemed immature for his age. He thought about becoming a teacher, and was enticed towards a small teacher's college that one of the student advisers had talked about where they were experimenting with small and informal classes. It was also publicized that the college had four girls to every boy.

Because of the friendship, Sid revealed inner thoughts and memories that he had not shared with anyone else.   One was his childhood dream of becoming a forest ranger. When he was seven, the family took a trip to Yellowstone National Park. He was captivated by a forest ranger they encountered. He was on a horse and posed a striking figure in an attractive uniform with a wide-brimmed hat with a leather chin strap. He represented a friendly and authoritative figure that captured the imagination of a young boy.

His domineering father would not agree to any teacher prospect, asserting that teachers made too little money for a man to have luxuries and to raise a family. It also carried little impression as a role model for his own children. Sid did not dare raise any possibility of a forest ranger as a career fearing an even more demonstrative objection. He insisted that Sid go to a large university and become a dentist. Because of the lack of any high and special credentials Sid could not get into an ivy league school and was only accepted at the State University. He was disinterested and poor at science subjects and flunked out in the first year. Even a social life on the large campus was disappointing. With the disgrace and disappointment of his father, further education was out of the question and he went out on his own. He considered joining the army but was not comfortable with that prospect. The early dream of becoming a forest ranger was too fleeting and nebulous for him to grasp and best relegated to the compartment in a lost life of what might have been. He had a series of manual jobs until he finally settled in a job as an insurance clerk with repetitive and boring work assignments.

Sid married the first woman who showed an interest in him, and he did not find out until after they were married that she was not really interested in him but was trying to escape from a bad family situation.   Mandy did not love him, and her true qualities surfaced quickly. She demanded constant attention and insisted he create social situations where she could be with other people, preferably new people so that she could retell the same exaggerated personal stories. It drove him crazy as it was always the same, and the irony of it was that she was the only one who enjoyed the mundane stories. A particularly grating and insensitive feature of her personality was a gushing sweetness with others while she would treat

Vain Regrets

and speak to him with disdain and irritability.   She was frigid in bed and withheld sexual favors as a form of punishment and dissatisfaction. Mandy constantly criticized and belittled him, and would complain to others how little money he made and would not take her anywhere. She refused to get a job and spent the day watching television, smoking, and drinking. When she went out shopping she bought expensive items many of which were never worn or used. Once she bought a very expensive custom-made sofa that he thought was hideous. It took him three years to pay it off. For him, this was a constant discovery and reinforcement of evilness that colored his entire outlook and behavior. It curtailed any desire to do things and to interact with people. It was as if all will was sapped from his being.

With Roger's stimulation to think, one event that occurred during the marriage came back to him that had been buried in the deep recesses of his mind, and he wondered if it would have made a difference in his life if he had reacted differently. Perhaps, it had been a minor turning point. A young couple down the street invited them over one evening for dessert. The wife, Dorene, was beautiful and a champion tennis player. The husband, John, was handsome, clever, and a Harvard graduate. He was being groomed to take over his father's industrial corporation. They already had plans drawn for a custom home to be built in an upscale neighborhood.   Their two young children were as perfect as the parents. When they were eating the dessert, Sid was sitting with Dorene on one side of the table while Mandy was sitting with John on the other side. As usual, Mandy was expounding on one of her long-winded obscure personal stories. Suddenly, Dorene pressed her leg against his leg. He was bewildered. Was she not aware of what she was doing, or was it a sensitive reaction of sympathy in recognition of what he was putting up with? Or, was it something more? About a month later, Sid was shopping at the grocery store and Dorene was there shopping with the children. When she saw him, she came up to him and gave him a big hug. She told him that she and John had separated, and that she was still in the house but John had moved out. She reached in her handbag and pulled out a piece of paper and a pen. She wrote her telephone number down, gave it to him, and asked him to call her. He thought about doing that many times and actually picked up the telephone several times, but he never did. He was just so intimidated by his oppressive wife that he was terrified what she would say and do if she caught him. That was its own form of a lasting painful agony.

After two years, Mandy ran off with who he believed was a gambler. It was a relief of sorts, and Sid was better off alone. However, he had already withdrawn from the world around him. He had seen Dorene from a distance at one time and she was with a new man, and then she had moved away. Female companionship alluded him and the few overtures he made were greeted with rejection. He could not sustain a conversation with men long enough to raise interest in a friendship. Disillusionment with the present colored the future. Sure, he felt sorry for himself. Nobody else would.

Roger had said all people make poor choices from time to time. Sid countered that there is really little consolation in the concept that misery loves company. Roger made constant efforts to uplift his spirits but Sid knew that was too big a job even for an author.

At least fixing on a turning point led him to a better understanding of the failures and weaknesses. He was sure that if a turning point led to a turning back of the clock, all would have been different. There would be no assurance it would have been better, but it was inconceivable that it could have been any worse.

By focusing on this turning point, Sid also languished in the mind game of what might have been. He had not been much of a dreamer realizing he had little to dream about. Now, it seemed as if dreams took control of his thinking, and he wondered to the point of exasperation what it would have been like and how different things might have been if he had gone to the teacher's college. Besides a distinct lack of scholastic and subject pressure, he envisioned easing into the dating process if only by the sheer number of females without boyfriends. He even conjured up a sweet young girl and they learned together the ecstasy of young love. Despite Roger's pronouncement that there is no such thing as never and always, Sid had never experienced a genuine emotional and consuming love. Chances would have been greater to find that where he had not been.

For sure, if he had known then, he would have sought out a slew of authors early in his life. An author is the best medicine. An author can lead a reader on a pathway the reader would not dare to travel alone. Yes, if Sid had it all to do over again, he would be a teacher and an author. Then vain regrets might only be fiction.

FOUR

Roger was the only real friend he ever had. Sid fully realized what he had missed not having a friend in life. A friend is a person to confide in and to share the obvious as well as personal confidences. A friend is a person to seek advice from and solicit opinions, as well as one to soothe the hurts along the way and smooth out the bumps in the road. It is said that a friend is a person who knows you and wants to know you. Roger's reasoning and the impact of his books left Sid with a form of self power he had not had before. That was the capacity and the desire to dream. It was not possible to relive his life, but he could dream he was reliving it.

The dreams at night were not clear and often disconnected. The recollection was not complete and details lacking. During the day it was different. After his lunch tray was taken away, he would settle into the easy chair by the window, put his feet up on the ottoman, and for an hour or an hour and a half he was submerged in the world of yesteryear. Vivid images projecting actual feelings and emotions he was sure he no longer had surfaced and registered in his mind and heart. It was nearly a continuing personal soap opera.

Randolph Teachers College was set twelve miles from a quaint town. A hilly terrain separated the small male dormitory from the two larger female dormitories, the dining hall, and the classroom buildings. Between the dining hall and each female dormitory was a bridge.

On the day of Sid's arrival at the college, his roommate had not yet checked in, so he leisurely unpacked. He glanced in the mirror above the dresser he had picked out and stared at the eighteen-year-old face that reflected back to him. The deep set hazel eyes in a long and narrow face below a bushy head of curly brown hair was a sight to digest. A slightly crooked nose above thin lips completed the picture of a less than noteworthy figure. Yet, he was undaunted and determined to derive full benefits from this new adventure. If only his spirit was visible.

His roommate, Josh DeWald, was a pleasant and considerate person so they hit it off from the start. Josh was more outgoing, and Sid suspected he was at the college more for the social life than the teaching career design.

The classes were small and informal just as advertised. Sid probably would not have noticed Jennette Willoboughy with so many other prettier and more vivacious girls swirling around, but she was the only girl that was in all of the same classes. Short black hair with bangs down to her glasses and large black eyes capped a petite frame. Thin lips and a short stubby nose and slightly puffy lips were not the composite of a beauty queen, although he would glance at her frequently sensing there was a hidden beauty behind the common disguise.

They did not speak to one another until the first Friday night social, the socials held in the dining hall lobby. She approached him and was the first to speak, a soft voice accentuating the impression of buried treasures. "I know you are Sidney, the echo person in all of my classes." The smile was warm and the dimples distinctive. "Formally, I am Jennette, but I am usually called Jenny."

He shook the hand extended towards him and found the small hand to be warm and soft. "I guess we are stuck with each other. Call me Sid or Sidney." He hoped she liked the smile that came easily to his lips as he looked into the black eyes behind her glasses. She smiled back so that was encouragement enough.

She glanced out the lobby windows before speaking. "Sure is raining hard tonight."

His response probably sounded inane. "I suppose that is why there are so few students here tonight."

He did not display much of a sense of humor, although Jenny would prove numerous times that she had enough for both of them. "It is raining cats and dogs. There is a prohibition about having pets on campus so I wonder where they will all wind up."

"I have a large umbrella which should come in handy tonight. It is waterproof but not animal proof."

The social ended at 7:45. Girls had an eight o'clock curfew every night except Saturday when it was ten o'clock. They talked until that closing moment to the exclusion of others around them. The more they talked, the more pleasurable it became. If thoughts and feelings ran in tandem, this was a prime example.

Since he had that large umbrella, he walked her back to her dormitory. They were silent during the walk, the rain pounding on the umbrella as if it was was an aquatic symphony accompanying each step. She held on to his arm firmly, and it felt comforting to him. Once across the quaint wooden bridge, they agreed to meet at the dining hall in the morning to have breakfast. After she entered the door to the lobby she turned and waved to him. It was a sincere gesture and it was accompanied by a warm smile. He stared after her long after she was out of sight.

Nap time was over, and as his eyes gradually opened, it was of particular significance that rain was lashing against the window producing a sound similar to the one on the umbrella. He stayed in the chair enjoying the warm sensations that spread through his body. Any feeling was new to him, and the aftermath of the dream was especially welcome. He could hardly wait to see Jenny again.

FIVE

The next day brought the continuation he was looking forward to. He had only nibbled at the lunch on the tray, and the attendant inquired if he was ill when she took it away. As a thankful tribute to old age, the nap came quickly.

Jenny was waiting when he entered the dining hall. Her smile drew him to her side and they proceeded through the cafeteria line. They seemed to have much to discuss as they ate at a table off to the side, both totally oblivious to other students coming and going.

It was obvious they were a matched pair, and they accepted the emotional fact that they were inseparable as the natural order of things. Since part of the informality of the classes was that the students did not have assigned seats and could sit wherever they wanted to, in each class they sat next to each other. They ate all meals together, usually just the two of them, but occasionally joined by Josh or Deana Smythe, Jenny's roommate. Boys were allowed in the lobby of a girl's dormitory until the curfew, so they studied together there. They partnered whenever a project was designed for that. They would attend the Friday night socials, leaving early to walk along the paths or to sit on a bench. On Saturday nights, the college showed a movie, and as they watched in the dark hand would be clutched to hand.

Neither one had ever had a romantic relationship before, and they reveled in the newness of each sensation and every reward. Sid amazed himself in the extent of affection he was capable of and inspired to. Jenny was enthralled by the passion that took steady hold of the relationship. Repetitive hugs and kisses abounded, with ardent kisses prevalent in moments of privacy. On each night they would linger on the bridge for a special kiss goodnight. Constant proclamations of love accompanied their quiet moments, and they explored their bodies through their clothing as a special manifestation of the love they shared. Jenny was fully aware of his arousal when they embraced extensively. The first time he caressed the mounds on her chest, she instinctively drew back. "You might as well know now because you will find out for yourself. Those are not real. I stuff my bra with tissues. I am as flat chested as they come. Maybe, I was supposed to be a boy. Anyway, when they were giving out breasts there was either a shortage or I was thrown out of line because I did not have an appointment."

His initial reaction was to laugh at her wit, but thinking that basically she might be very sensitive about it all he held her tightly. "It is inconsequential to me. I am a leg man, and you have gorgeous legs. I think you are perfect no matter what. I love you with or without."

She returned his embrace with a fervent tug. He must have said all the right things. "Rest assured I have all of the other vital female parts and they are fully functional."

Jenny stopped wearing a bra and basked in a freedom from what others might think. The one that mattered had glossed over a problem she had wrestled with for years, or at least a problem she thought she had to wrestle with because of the weird concept society puts on sexual allure. One night as they kissed he slipped a hand under her sweater and was able to fondle the nub of a nipple rising erect from her chest. Her moan of satisfaction was reward enough.

The holidays were hard on them to be apart. They talked at length each night on the telephone. It was significant that there was so much to talk about. The reunions were joyous celebrations.

Sid did not want to awaken from this nap as it was so enjoyable, but the moment caught up with him. It amazed him how real it all had been. It gave him a new insight into how Roger's imagination make his characters so real. He made a note on the pad on the table to tell Roger that the next time they spoke. He showed the note to Jenny not for her approval but so that she would know everything he did and thought. That is how real she had become to him. A dream can be larger and better than life.

SIX

Added satisfaction came in just thinking abut the dreams. Telling Roger all of the details of each dream was another form of reliving them and produced further enjoyment of them. Sid was basking in a life he suspected existed but was not sure about. It was a magical transformation from an eighty-year existence void of emotional sensations to a feelings adventure.

While each nap did lead to a dream, it was not always a continuation of the one close to his heart. Yet, each other dream had at its core an achievement or a situation in which he was in control, elements missing in the real past. In one dream, at the insurance company he was put in charge of a promotional task force with a dozen employees assigned to work under him. In another, it revolved around the evil wife. Instead of her leaving him, he demonstrably told her off and walked out on her.

When the coveted dream did recur, the first academic year had been completed successfully. Sid and Jenny worked for the summer as counselors at an eight week sleep away camp for children. There they had the privacy and freedom to engage in a first and later physical unions to match the coupling of their hearts. When the weather was favorable and they were not assigned to do night patrol of the bunks, with blanket in hand they went to the back of the archery range. A row of tall pines provided a comfortable layer of pine needles. There was loving joy in undressing each other and bodies would meld on the blanket. Undisturbed and unhurried moments led to the discovery of maximizing pleasure. It was young love as old as the ages.

During the day at the camp there was ample opportunity to partake and observe how they reacted with children. Jenny wanted to have a large family as she now knew she had so much love to share. They talked often about being married and what it would be like. There were the prospects of teaching together. Raising a family would be a joy in the loving atmosphere they were establishing.

This had been a most satisfying dream, and Sid would not mind if it was repeated. It was not, however, and actually its substance raised a further somewhat disturbing dream. Because of the profusion of love and the increasing discussions of plans to marry after graduation, the families started to think that the relationship was getting too serious. Both sets of parents thought they were too immature and inexperienced to settle on a permanent mate. The families conspired to discourage the relationship. Jenny's parents even went so far as to prohibit her from seeing him any more. Jenny's adamant opposition to that idea, including a threat of suicide, and the parents backed down.

Instead of dissuading the couple, such opposition just made their resolve stronger. Nothing and no one would break apart what they knew was a perfect whole.

Sid awoke from that nap and was sweating profusely. Anger and fortitude were welcome additions to his emotional inventory. It amazed him that after eighty-years of having little or no emotional responses to events and people, there was now a geyser of feelings with the capability of taking him to tremendous heights. He was in a new world, no doubt about that.

SEVEN

The more Sid described the intimacies of his dreams, the more Roger found himself curious if the same thing might work for him. It does not take much to get an author's imagination in high gear. As much as he rationalized over the years that his own regrets were actually turning points and that he had learned significant and lasting lessons from the episodes, he became consumed by wonder that if he let his imagination truly run free would it funnel into his dreams? Would he be able to dream the regrets away?

He tried everything he could think of to dream about that upsetting time period in his life when he was so cruel to Regina Stern. Before getting into bed, he would concentrate on all of the hurtful and mean details of his behavior with her. That was painful enough. That did not lead to any dreams about her. Then he tried to make a list of actions he should have taken to avoid the hurtful and mean acts. That did not lead to a dream to possibly relive that excruciating event of his past.

It was only after he stopped trying to initiate a dream did he actually dream of her. In vivid detail was her petite and slender form. The long brown hair had a sheen that he remembered well, and the wide brown eyes sparkled as she looked intently at him. The endearing smile on the thin lips meant just for him was evident. But, that is all there was. He could not force in the dream a different reaction to her advances or even a kind mannerism on his part. His writer's imagination could be molded to bring plot or character to life and control the direction of the story. He was unable to do that in a dream. It had been just her image fleeting by as if it were a cloud. Rather than a calming sensation he was seeking, he awoke agitated and weary with a form of disgust for himself. He hoped he would not dream of her again, and it had not happened since. Of course, that did not mean it could not happen and it did not mean it would give him an opportunity to right a wrong even if it was just a dream. Uncertainty is one of an author's enemies.

His penance was in helping Sid and others like him to turn away from the burden of past regrets. His books were replete with that philosophy, out there for anyone who cared to read and think about it. He would leave the magic of erasing regrets by reliving those aspects of past lives in dreams to Sid and the others who might have the capacity to do so.

EIGHT

Most likely influenced by the love story of the characters of Stanley and Cindy in *Glimpses of the Past* who had been teachers, catapulted through time and Sid's next dream had the two lovers graduated and teaching together in an elementary school just outside a large city. It did not take long for them to become recognized as special teachers. Parents appreciated the value of their children having superior influences, and the children flocked around the two wherever they went as if they were dispensing candy. Sid and Jenny loved them all, and hugs seemed to be the best part of everyone's day.

They rented a small house about a twenty minute drive from the school until they could save enough to buy a home and start raising a family. The house was comfortable, and with deep woods behind it, lovely gardens and lots of stepping stones, it peaked all of their romantic inclinations. Dining on the private back porch was a favorite activity. In the evenings they would sit at the dining room table doing lesson plans, grading papers, and talk over all sorts of novel and creative ways to get the children to learn through play and outlets for their growing imagination.

Life can be good in both reality and dreams. Too often it does not stay that way. Perhaps, it is just a reminder that there are many factors that interplay to keep it that way. Perhaps, it is just the acknowledgment that the variety and extent of conditions, events, and personalities can alter the status in an instant.

Sid died in his sleep. Roger hoped that the final dream he was having sealed the contentment experienced at the end of his life. No matter how brief the period was, Sid found a fresh human experience to offset the lack of such insights earlier. His regrets were not completely in vain.

Sid must have known that death was near because he had prepared for it. Roger's books were in a box on the table with a note stating that Roger should be contacted and given the box.

When Roger picked up the box, he sat on the terrace under the elm tree where the two men had so many conversations. He opened the envelope in the box that was addressed to him.

> Roger, my dear friend:
>
> When you read this I will be but a memory.
> I hope it is a pleasant one and that I adequately
> fulfilled my job as Vice President. Our friendship
> and your books filled my last days with a
> contentment I was unable to achieve in my
> early life. Best of all, they empowered me to
> dream a life I did not have. Thank you for
> you and for them. I hope you will be able to
> do the same wonder for another old timer who
> has vain regrets. Remember me kindly.
>
> Sid

There was another envelope in the box. It was addressed to Jenny. Roger was not sure why he hesitated opening it. Perhaps, he felt it was a form of infringing on their privacy, a sign of disrespect for their love. He was sure, however, that Sid expected him to read it.

> Jenny, my love —
>
> As a woman of my dreams you became real to
> me, more real than so many of the actual
> experiences I had endured. You are the love
> I always wanted and, if I would have had it,
> instead of regrets over the years there would
> have been a lasting contentment. My true
> happiness would have been in loving you

and sharing in the accomplishments that
would have become warm memories. As in
life, you will be my dream love in death.
That way it will be forever.

Your Sid

Roger was convinced that Sid was basically an exceptional person and that it was unfortunate that he did not believe that in himself until so late. Roger had told him in various ways that he was worthy of being a character in one of his books. A gentle breeze brushed along his cheek. It was nice to think that was a sign that Sid agreed with him. It was then and there that Roger decided to actually make Sid a character in a new book. In fact, he would be a main character as it would be a book of the story of his dream. That way the dream would carry on.

As many books as he had written, Roger felt a burst of unusual excitement in starting this writing. A man making his own world would be a story worth telling. Hopefully, it would also be a story worth reading.

IN HIS WORLD

A Dream Story of an Idyllic Love

by

ROGER KIMBEL

Go confidently in the direction of your dreams! Live the life you've imagined.

— Henry David Thoreau

This book is a work of fiction. However, it is based on a true story, but not in the sense one usually relates to that term. It is true because a character was real and in his final days to offset a life of regrets he lived in a world he made in his dreams. That world could have been and should have been his real world. For the purposes of this story, it was.

ONE

It is not easy being a teenager at any time period. It was especially problematic in the 1950s when the term *teenager* began to be used with frequency to describe an age group that is neither here nor there. Floundering between childhood and adulthood, as an entity teenagers in the 1950s were seeking a distinct and significant identity. Teenagers were developing trends uniquely their own, be it music, language, and fashion. It was a particularly difficult time for a teenager who did not fit in and did not belong emotionally to the rising tide.

Sidney Corwin was chronologically a teenager, but in many ways he was left behind in the rush towards group identity. Probably, the main cause of his basic immaturity and failure to act or partake in the changing cultural landscape was because he was an only child of a doting mother and a domineering father. The parents were constantly at cross purposes concerning Sidney's upbringing. It also did not help that his self image was in dire straits. While he would get a growth spurt when he was sixteen, at fourteen when he started high school in 1951 he was very short. His features were not anything special so as to be noticed, and a full head of unruly curly brown hair raised the image that the body beneath the head was also out of control. As such, adults and those in his own age group avoided him. He was unable to sustain a conversation and did not like any physical activities, so he had no friends. He did not care for school or studying, and only an innate intelligence sustained him.

Sidney in 1954 as a senior struggled to have a say in a college decision. His father had already made it clear that Sidney should go to a large university and become a dentist. Sidney balked at that as having no interest or aptitude in science subjects and envisioning it being disgusting putting his hands in other people's mouths. He had no idea what he wanted to do with his life even if he had one. An early childhood fantasy of becoming a forest ranger was lost in the rush and crush of reality. Yet, that image emerged at rare times, and it still represented a goal of freedom and adventure. Some goals are unattainable. He felt he had no choice but to accept that, and it made him even more disgruntled.

He saw some literature in the Guidance Office describing Randolph Teacher's College, and he thought it sounded good when it described small and informal classes and a ratio of four females to each male. In a smaller class setting he might not feel overwhelmed. If he was ever to have a girlfriend, he needed this kind of favorable odds.

Family arguments ensued after his announcement that he wanted to go to Randolph. His father urged that teachers make a woefully low salary and that Sidney would never be able to raise a family on such a meager sum. He would probably not even be able to afford a house, a car, or a television. Further, a teacher would be a poor financial model if he had sons. His doting mother finally convinced his father to let Sidney try it for a year just for the experience and then transfer to a larger university to major in a more productive prospect.

In a different city in 1951, a fourteen-year-old girl starting high school was in a similar resulting situation. Jennette Willoboughy was ignored in a family with seven children and spurned by other children in the neighborhood as being ugly and awkward. Her very poor eyesight was discovered later than it should have been, and she had been wearing glasses with thick lenses since age six. Clothing did not seem to fit her right, and she shunned using any makeup that other girls were starting to use. Above all else, while other girls her age were developing breasts, she remained as flat chested as she was as a little girl. That would not change throughout high school, and it was only when an older sister showed her how to pad her chest did her plain looks get even a short glance from the boys. Her mother refused to take her to a doctor for examination exclaiming that development sometimes comes later and it would catch up with her. It did not happen, and she resigned herself to it rather than continuously brood about it. There was no close friend to confide in, and the sisters were too busy to listen. Gradually, she withdrew further and further into herself.

In her senior year, 1954, career and college choices arose. Her father was a successful business manager, and money was available to send all of the children to college. Jennette had few options as the times offered restricted viable choices. Girls still concentrated on the prospects of marriage and family and while biding their time popular occupational choices were as nurses, teachers, secretaries, or librarians. For Jennette marriage and family were a distant hope. Actually, she strongly wanted to become a teacher ever since fourth grade when Mrs. Roberts paid special attention to her and fostered a thirst for learning. She believed she could accomplish that same end, and she also loved children as they were not as judgmental as her peers. So, for what she considered a history of discomfort as an outsider, it was a ray of bright light in the decision to go to Randolph Teacher's College. As a prelude to the exciting prospect, she asked her family to call her Jenny instead of Jennette.

TWO

Randolph Teacher's College was located in a pastoral setting ten miles from the nearest town in Virginia. On one edge of the grounds was a relatively small male dormitory. A dining hall separated that housing facility from the two larger female dormitories. A stream ran between the dining room and the residences for the women, and there were two rustic wooden bridges spanning the stream towards each dormitory. The students long ago started calling them the kissing bridges as they were relatively dark at night and private so as to be a good place for a couple to kiss before the girl entered the dormitory. Set on a hill beyond these dormitories were the classroom buildings, the library, and further off the faculty housing followed by acres of woods.

Only seniors were allowed to have automobiles, and there were few that did. Since the college was distant from the town, it provided its own social events. There was a tea, cookies, and sandwich social every Friday night in the dining hall lobby from 6:00 P.M. to 7:45 P.M., and a movie shown in the same place on Saturday nights at 7:30. Girls had an 8:30 P.M. curfew except on Saturday night when it was 10:00 P.M. Boys had an 11:00 P.M. curfew every night.

Jenny's roommate, Deana Smythe, was already there the day she arrived. As Jenny would have guessed, Deana was in startling contrast to her as being tall, blonde, and with an ample bosom. However, these qualities did not affect the warm and considerate person she was, probably mostly due to her small town upbringing. Deana hugged her right away. Later, upon discovering Jenny's lack of chest development, her comment was endearing: "Makes no difference to me and won't to the right guy either." Jenny felt at ease and with a set direction finally in her life she was basically content. That was a novelty.

Sidney arrived before his roommate, Josh DeWald. He unpacked and took an exploratory walk to the dining hall. The lobby was large with numerous tables and chairs, and an entire wall lined with a bank of student mailboxes. He took a deep breath and resolved to make this undertaking work not only to show his parents that this was a better decision but also because the idea of becoming a teacher was gaining greater appeal for his future.

Josh was pleasant and considerate, and the two of them got along from the start. Sid was pleased that he could converse with Josh with such ease. Josh was quick to admit he was there for the social life more than for a career as a teacher, but time would prove otherwise.

Meals in the dining hall were served cafeteria-style with each student possessing an annual meal ticket. Sid and Josh went for their first meal which they found better than they expected, and they were certainly distracted by all of the pretty and vivacious girls milling around. The girls looked mostly at Josh, and he was in his glory. Sidney did catch a quick glance or two, and he was encouraged by seeing all of these female forms. There just had to be one for him among that throng!

Since the classes were small as publicized, Sid was able to scrutinize which other students were in each class. He had five classes the first day, and by the third class he noted that Jenny was the only other student in each class so far. She was not nearly as pretty as many of the other girls, but he liked that she wore glasses as he did, and he liked her movements as he occasionally observed her. Since he considered himself different from others, there was an aura about her that indicated she was unlike others as well.

It turned out that they were together in all of the classes. They did not speak but did nod to one another to acknowledge that fact.

It was at the Friday night social that they had a first talk. It was raining quite hard that night and the turnout was small. Sidney was standing off to the side as Josh went off with two girls to partake of the food. As she approached him she smiled, and he quickly looked down and noticed her shapely legs beneath the short skirt. Her bosom stood out in the tight sweater. She was very short and had long straight black hair. Her bangs came down to the top of her glasses. He could barely tell that her eyes were black through the thick lenses.

Jenny was not sure where the bravery came from for her to approach a boy, but perhaps it was just another new part of her transformation. "Hi," she smiled again. "You are my class shadow. Your name is Sidney, isn't it? I am Jennette, although I prefer Jenny."

He shook the small and warm hand extended towards him and reluctantly let it go after a few seconds. It had the sensation of holding a hand, an act he thought about often but had not yet experienced. "Sid will do for me. We may be the only two in the same classes." It sounded trite and he almost wished he could take back the words. Unaccustomed to talking to a girl and not really knowing how to impress one, it was probably close to a miracle that he was able to speak at all.

Jenny had a wonderful sense of humor. It was just that she had few opportunities in her guarded life to let it show. She would prove that over and over again as time would pass, even inspiring Sid to be free speaking which was far afield from his nature. "As my class shadow, you must take notes for me if I miss a class at shadow pay which I calculate is hardly there."

He liked the dimples in her cheeks when she smiled. "Likewise."

"It's raining cats and dogs out there. Since no pets are allowed, I wonder what they are going to do with all of them."

The humor alluded him, but he would learn. "I never had a dog."

"Me neither, but it would be nice some day."

He had not wanted a pet as a child, but it occurred to him as he thought about it that he might have missed out on something. "Would you like to get some tea and sit at a table?"

"Sure."

They went to the long buffet table and picked up the cups of tea and put some of the cookies and small sandwiches on a plate. They sat and talked until the end of the social.

He had a large umbrella and offered to walk her back to her dormitory. The rain beat down on the umbrella as an aquatic symphony accompanying their steps. She clutched his arm to get under the umbrella as much as possible. That felt good to him. Actually, he felt good all over. They did not speak until they crossed the bridge when they arranged to meet for breakfast. He walked her to the lobby door so she would not get wet. Once inside, she turned, waved, and smiled. He felt as if his heart was melting. He stared until she was out of sight.

His shoes were soaked by the time he got back to the room. He hardly noticed. Josh was already there and Sid told him about Jenny and what a good time he had with her. Josh winked, "Sounds like love to me."

Jenny could hardly contain her excitement and she told Deana all the details. Deana chuckled. "Here just a week and you are in love already. These teacher boys move fast."

THREE

Jenny was waiting just outside the main door to the dining room. Without hesitation they hugged, neither sure or concerned about who initiated it. Reluctantly, they broke apart and went through the food line.

They ate at a table off to the side totally oblivious to students around them. While finishing the coffee in the cups, Sid reached across the table and clasped her hand. She responded with a squeeze. Not caring if others overheard, he spoke slowly. "Last night was special because of being with you."

She smiled. "It's not fair taking words out of my mouth."

He continued as if no force could hold him back. "Do you believe in love at first sight?"

She smiled again. "No, but I do believe in love at first social."

It was his turn to smile. He intertwined his fingers with hers, and it seemed as familiar as if they had done that many times. "Before I came here, I thought I would never find love. I never had a girl friend. I have never even kissed a girl."

"This is a teacher's college. I'll teach you that if I knew about it myself. I never kissed a boy, never had a boy friend. Not even close."

Part of the informality of the classes was not assigning seats to the students and allowing them to sit where they wanted to. The pair sat next to one another in all of the classes. They held hands walking to and from each class. They had all of their meals together, usually just the two of them but occasionally joined by Josh or Deana.

It was after the next social that they shared a first kiss on the bridge. The days were getting shorter as autumn settled in so it was dark on the bridge. They had left the function a little early so that it would be as private as possible on the bridge. First, they kissed with their glasses on, proclaiming they wanted to see everything even though their eyes were closed. Then, they tried it without glasses, concluding that either way it was magical. A wonderful vent for two people starved for love and confirming a strong belief harbored in their hearts that they had so much love to give.

It was warm and beautiful on Sunday. Only two meals were served on Sundays, breakfast and a bountiful lunch. After lunch they explored the grounds of the college. Beyond the faculty housing they discovered trails through the woods. The leaves were turning vivid colors and birds singing was the only noise. It was the beginning of another kind of love for people who lived in a city, and they embraced this love of nature with enthusiasm. It was evident that they had much to learn about nature and were eager to do so. They planned to take books out from the library on trees, plants, and birds.

They lingered in a place sheltered by the vegetation and kissed with passion. She felt his arousal against her and it pleased her that he reacted to her that way. He put his hand under her sweater. She shuddered and drew back. "You might as well know now because you are going to find out. Those are not real. I stuff my bra with tissues. I am totally flat chested. When they were giving out breasts they either ran out of them by the time I got to the head of the line or they threw me out of the line because I did not have an appointment. Anyway, I do it because our sexually crazed society expects women to have bosoms and the bigger the better."

His initial reaction was to laugh at her wit, but he thought she might be sensitive about it. "Makes no difference to me. I am a leg man, and you have magnificent legs. Besides, I was starting to think you were perfect, so this takes some of the pressure off. I love you with or without."

He must have said the right thing because she hugged him forcefully. "Rest assured all of my other female parts are there and as far as I can tell fully functional."

Hand-in-hand they walked all of the trails, delighting in the beauty and peace of it all. Love is not blind. Rather, it opens eyes in new and exciting ways. The significance and amazing contrast between a state of love between two people and the immense world of nature was something they would experience and talk about often. Instead of a conflict, the two loves were compatible and even complemented each other.

FOUR

Jenny stopped wearing a bra and experienced a new sense of freedom in doing so. It mattered not to the one she loved, and it made her proud to shun one of the confining dictates society invented. Deana applauded the revolution.

Boys were allowed in the lobby of a girl's dormitory until curfew, so they would go from supper to Jenny's dormitory and study until close to curfew time. They would make sure to leave ample time to go out to the bridge for a kiss goodnight. The bridge had become a special symbol of their relationship. It stood as the spanning and uniting of their two worlds, and the sentimentality of good night kisses on such an edifice was an event to look forward to and to remember always. It also had a special place in their concept of nature. They talked often of having in their own home some day within an area of vegetation a rustic wooden bridge to mark this early romance. A togetherness that creates and stores warm memories becomes impervious.

Before all of the leaves fell, they walked the woods often with books in hand to study all that greeted them. The abundance and variety amazed them, and the more they knew the more entranced they became.

It snowed the week before the Thanksgiving break. That was another new and wondrous experience as they trudged through the same trails that were now snow covered.

Separation at the breaks for Thanksgiving, Christmas, between semesters, and at spring were difficult. The comfort was in being together. Yet, they managed to talk on the telephone every day they were apart, and both agreed it was meaningful that they managed to have so much to talk about.

The families suspected something serious was going on, but Sid and Jenny were not going to get the families involved at this point. They knew for certain there would be all sorts of opposition since they would not be taken seriously. After all, they were only eighteen, had never dated before, and were limited in social situation experiences. Better to let time solidify their stance.

By the end of the first school year, both had excelled academically and were on the Dean's List. Studying nature was a plus on their own, and it was glorious to be part of the process in the woods as the spring emerged. It seemed that the more they knew about nature the more they wanted to know.

During the summer break, they worked as counselors at a full summer camp for children in Massachusetts. Sid had a bunk of ten-year-old boys; Jenny had a bunk of eight-year-old girls. If not involved with scheduled activities, they took the children on nature walks. It was uplifting and inspiring to arouse the interest of the children in the matters they studied and could explain fully. Fascination about nature is easily transferable. The children especially liked making leaf albums. Sid and Jenny knew this was solid preparation for them as teachers and parents. One important observation they took away from this camp experience was that it is important to listen to children when they express themselves, and it is vital to encourage such communications. Other lessons digested were that humor can be an excellent way of disciplining and children soak up affection. Each also observed how they reacted with children, fueling the future confidence of raising their own family.

They easily became the most popular counselors at the camp. While other bunk leaders were anxious to leave their charges at bedtime to spend some time on their own, Sid and Jenny would hold back and each night tell or read stories to the children. That too had great rewards since they were able to gauge what peaked and sustained the imagination of the youngsters. That was probably nothing they could learn at the college.

After fully tucking the children into bed, if they were not on night patrol of the bunk areas, on pleasant and warm nights they would take a blanket to the back of the archery range where there was a secluded place with a thick layer of pine needles from the towering pine trees above. The blanket would be spread out on nature's bed and they would partake in a favorite game. They would undress each other, and in this peaceful setting bodies would meld in a loving attempt to catch up to the union of hearts and minds. Each time they made love it was a renewal and a confirmation.

At the beginning of the last week, color war was declared at the camp for three days. The camp was divided into a red team and a green team to compete in an array of sport activities with a final sing on the last night. Sid and Jenny were made opposing generals but that sort of rivalry just brought on new sparks of admiration for their qualities and a greater depth to their relationship. Each day was a growing up as well as a growing together.

FIVE

As they started the second year at the college, Jenny decided she wanted to be called Jen so they would both have three-letter names. At registration, they made sure they were in all of the same classes.

The college was trying something new this year. No classes were scheduled during the last hour on Wednesdays, and that time could be used as extra study time or for club activities. The students were encouraged to form a club of interest and a faculty member would be assigned to oversee the activity and a classroom assigned for the meetings.

Sid and Jen put in a request to form a Nature Club. The increasing interest and love for nature had also led them to an activist position in promoting and protecting actions for the sustaining and development of the well-being of all phases of nature. They readily acknowledged that from a non-caring role in their younger years, they were seeking out causes that needed action to correct neglect, waste, or other wrongs.

The college, liberal in its current outlook, had just admitted the first Negro in the school's history. Most of the student body did not seem to care one way or another, but there was a vocal minority which protested and were attempting to make the young lady feel unwelcome. Sid and Jen decided to do something about it. It was yet another cause for them to participate in to right what they felt was a wrong or an injustice. They befriended Wilma Everett and had her join them at meals until the time she was more widely accepted and made additional friends on her own. At times, it takes a bold few to set the tone or good example for civility.

It was over the Christmas break that they exchanged home visits and broke the news that they planned to marry upon graduation. There was more strong opposition than they anticipated. Sid's parents were not receptive to this homely woman who showed little personality or responsiveness to suggestions that Sid had his entire life before him and should not be tied down to one kind of job or to one woman at this point. Bare emergence from a sheltered life is not the time to commit to anything. Sid's father still was hoping to prevail on him to seek more lucrative ambitions. Sid's mother injected enough of parental wisdom to keep on the sidelines at this time. After all, graduation was two and a half years away and any sort of distraction could turn the tide. Her mind raced to seek ideas of how to introduce Sid to more appealing women.

The opposition at Jen's home was even more pronounced. Perhaps because none of the other siblings had yet married, marriage was as yet not fully accepted. Her parents did not hesitate to express their opinion that Sid was nondescript. Her businessman father did not want her to marry a teacher who could not fully support her. Jen was given an ultimatum to either give up Sid or she would be pulled from the school. Jen was very upset. At Sid's suggestion she waited a few weeks but the parents did not relent. They did back off when they received Jen's letter stating that she would commit suicide if she could not be with Sid. The parents were nervous but decided similarly to Sid's family that anything could happen in the two and a half years to alter decisions and they would try more subtle approaches over that time.

The couple was not going to let the attitude of the families dampen their enthusiasm. After all, they were convinced this was right and the parents would eventually accept the inevitable. Opposition to a relationship can actually make that romance stronger.

Along with the celebration of their nineteenth birthdays, they reaffirmed their commitment to be lifelong partners. Such a vow was special and was another advance in the seriousness they attached to both the future career of teaching and marriage. Perhaps, the relationship might wind up to be the most significant activist position of them all.

SIX

For the summer they worked again as counselors at the children's camp. The owner of the camp was anxious to have them back and so many parents had inquired as to their return. Many of the same children were also signed up. Just as they loved each other, it was satisfying to know that the love spread to others was reciprocated.

As they started their junior year at the college, as was their established custom they began the academic year with a special kiss and embrace on the kissing bridge. They were still on the Dean's List which they attributed to their study habits and the continuing growth of serious intensity to their chosen career. This was accompanied by the ever-increasing interest and activity in causes that needed to be addressed. Their latest crusade was aimed at stopping the spread of atomic weapons. Since the Russian testing of a hydrogen bomb in 1953 and the United States resumption of atomic bomb testing in the desert areas in 1954, the world appeared to be on the brink of self-destruction. The thought that there might be no world left for them to teach in or to enjoy the fruits of their marriage was motivation enough, and they dreaded having to put the children in their classes through such drills as hiding under desks. There well might be no desks and no children. The cold war constantly raised the specter of hostile nation relations with possible horrendous consequences. Would the celebration of their twentieth birthdays be the last one? Would there be no future?

They established and headed the college chapter of SANE, Students Against Nuclear Experiments. There was plenty to do getting members and getting petitions signed, and they still did not neglect the Nature Club activities. Academically, it was another successful year, capped by a kiss on the kissing bridge on the last day of classes.

It was tempting to again return to the camp for the summer, but more serious options prevailed to satiate their activist incline. They took jobs as summer interns in the Washington, D.C. office of SANE. Pay was negligible although the rewards were in participating in lobbying Congress to have tests halted, to persuade the President to enter into nonproliferation agreements, and to establish new chapters of the organization in schools throughout the nation. There were some other personal benefits treasured by them. They were able to stay free in a small furnished apartment above a garage to the house of one of the senior staff members. It was as if they were married and living together without restrictions to their love and togetherness. It was in effect their first home.

It also gave them ample opportunity to reap the benefits of the culture and history that the nation's capitol had to offer. They went to every monument, government building, and museum, soaking in the significance and lessons offered. By far, their favorite site was the Library of Congress. The majestic Reading Room would alone be enough to captivate their interest and fuel a budding inspiration with the thirst for knowledge and warmth of books, but the Great Hall was icing on the cake. The awe inspiring beauty and preserved gems of civilization took their breath away. It filled them with hope, thoughts, and dreams. It became a game on the many visits to commit to memory many of the significant inscriptions and quotations etched around the ceiling and dome.

>THEY ARE NEVER ALONE THAT ARE ACCOMPANIED
>WITH NOBLE THOUGHTS

>ONE EQUAL TEMPER OF HEROIC HEARTS,
>MADE WEAK BY TIME AND FATE, BUT STRONG
>IN WILL TO STRIVE, TO SEEK, TO FIND,
>AND NOT TO YIELD

>BEAUTY IS TRUTH, TRUTH BEAUTY

>TOO LOW THEY BUILD WHO BUILD
>BENEATH THE STARS

Vain Regrets

THERE IS BUT ONE TEMPLE IN THE UNIVERSE
AND THAT IS THE BODY OF MAN

MAN RAISES, BUT TIME WEIGHS

THE NOBLEST MOTIVE IS THE PUBLIC GOOD

THE TRUE UNIVERSITY OF THESE DAYS IS A
COLLECTION OF BOOKS

THERE IS NO WORK OF GENIUS WHICH HAS NOT
BEEN THE DELIGHT OF MANKIND

IT IS THE MIND THAT MAKES THE MAN,
AND OUR VIGOR IS IN OUR MORTAL SOUL

TONGUES IN TREES, BOOKS IN THE RUNNING STREAMS,
SERMONS IN STONES, AND GOOD IN EVERYTHING

ONLY THE ACTIONS OF THE JUST SMELL SWEET
AND BLOSSOM IN THE DUST

LEARNING IS BUT AN ADJUNCT TO OURSELF

STUDIES PERFECT NATURE AND ARE
PERFECTED BY EXPERIENCE

DREAMS, BOOKS, ARE EACH A WORLD;
BOOKS WE KNOW, ARE A SUBSTANTIAL
WORLD, BOTH PURE AND GOOD

THE FAULT IS NOT IN OUR STARS BUT IN
OURSELVES, THAT WE ARE UNDERLINGS

Daniel Hill Zafren

CREATION'S HEIR, THE WORLD,
THE WORLD IS MINE!

VAIN, VERY VAIN, THE WEARY SEARCH TO FIND
THAT BLISS WHICH ONLY CENTRES IN THE MIND

IN NATURE ALL IS USEFUL, ALL IS BEAUTIFUL

ART IS LONG, AND TIME IS FLEETING

THE CHIEF GLORY OF EVERY PEOPLE
ARISES FROM ITS AUTHORS

MEMORY IS THE TREASURER AND GUARDIAN
OF ALL THINGS

THERE IS ONE ONLY GOOD, NAMELY, KNOWLEDGE;
AND ONE ONLY EVIL, NAMELY, IGNORANCE

KNOWLEDGE COMES, BUT WISDOM LINGERS

IN BOOKS LIES THE SOUL OF THE WHOLE PAST TIME

WORDS ARE ALSO ACTIONS AND ACTIONS
ARE A KIND OF WORDS

READING MAKETH A FULL MAN;
CONFERENCE A READY MAN; AND WRITING,
AN EXACT MAN

They took long walks along the Potomac River, and explored the parks. It would be nice if they wound up teaching here as the schools were in poor shape and the students woefully behind the national averages. The compelling need for teachers was obvious. Washington was an interesting cross between a large city and a small town. Once they graduated and overcame family opposition to the marriage, then they would delineate the options. The future beckoned, and they would be ready for it together.

SEVEN

It was bitter sweet as they kissed on the bridge to start the senior year. The years had been full and good, and it was poignant contemplating the end of this chapter of their lives. Perhaps, it was a special form of nostalgia as they had developed through the college years not only a potential as serious teachers but had gained a maturity about the value of living a meaningful life. It was the final launching point for their careers and the doorstop to a love in a world waiting to be conquered, assuming the competing nations of the world would allow the world to exist.

Josh, who must have dated half of the female population of the college without finding a serious female companion, came back from the summer break with an unexpected love interest. He had worked as a waiter at a hotel in the Catskills and to his amazement found the girl that sent his heart aflame. He had befriended one of the chambermaids, a kind and considerate woman from the local town. One day, she brought her daughter with her to help her with her rounds. It was love at first sight. Allison, who he immediately called Ally in spontaneous recognition that she would be his ally, although only sixteen was cute and a personal replica of her mother. He raved about her every virtue and had spent every nonworking moment with her. Josh found her thirst for life exhilarating and she was enchanted with all things that came her way. Perfect qualifications as Josh saw it for a teacher's wife. Sid was happy for him, and Josh was consumed once back at the college with writing love letters whenever he was not studying. He planned on finding a teaching job at the town she lived in to establish and perpetuate their magical discovery. He thought it would be no problem at all to get parental consent for a marriage he pictured as perfect as the one he predicted for Sid and Jen.

Deana, Jen's roommate, also had a depressing social life at the college. As beautiful as she was, few satisfying dates over the years had left her disappointed in the romance department. Jen repeatedly reassured her that a man worthy of her would come along but that was little comfort for the love starved. Deana had said more than once she would like a man half as attentive as Sid was.

Applications for teaching positions had to be completed before the end of the first semester. As much as they wanted to teach in the District of Columbia because they felt they could do much good there as well as enjoy the city, there was a rule that married teachers could not teach at the same school and that would defeat one of their fondest dreams. So, they had to explore seeking to work elsewhere. It seemed that large cities had the same sort of restriction so they began to concentrate on smaller cities and towns where there would also be a rustic form of life to give full vent to their love of nature. Because of their superior academic records and a slew of faculty recommendations they were accepted wherever they applied. The choice was narrowed between a town in Connecticut and one in Maryland.

After a visit to both areas, they chose the Connecticut location because the town was located on the shore of Candlewood Lake, a lake being developed by the power company that would be eleven miles long with over five thousand acres surface and have a proposed shoreline of eighty six miles. With the lake, it was bound to be a thriving area with many families locating there because of the scenic beauty and recreational potential. The schools should be full. The pull of the nature input was strong for them as well. A love of nature had become as strong as the desire to teach.

After graduation they married in a simple civil ceremony with only immediate family and Josh and Deana present. It was a mere formality since they had considered themselves married for all the years of their togetherness. Contrary to the earlier schemes by the families to divide the couple, they actually came to accept what was accentuated time and time again as inevitable. Jen's father, figuring he was saving a bundle by not paying for a large wedding, gave the couple as a wedding present a lot on what was to be a hidden cove at Candlewood Lake that he was able to get though his business connections at even a better price than advertised predevelopement prices. The couple loved the lot and easily pictured a home there in the future with even more than one kissing bridge.

They rented a fully furnished log cabin a few miles from the elementary school at which Sid would be teaching sixth grade and Jen fourth grade. It had gardens and woods behind it and would be a satisfactory temporary home while they saved for the dream house. Good things come to good people. They believed that and were sure it would prove true continuously.

EIGHT

At some point in time all love probably gets tested. A great love may be subject to a greater test. Such a test can come in many ways. It can be challenged by other persons or even by society. It can be undermined by heart or mind of either one or both of the lovers. It can be stressed by facts or circumstances purposely imposed or by ones unpredicted and unexpected.

Things seemed calm and normal. Sid and Jen were comfortable and content in the rental home, and even the furnishings while not ones they would have chosen were adequate. Daily school events were uneventful and pleasant enough, and they had established good relationships with the children and other teachers and administrators. The children eagerly awaited the engaging learning techniques the new teachers displayed.

Towards the end of October one of Jen's younger sisters, Florence, telephoned them one night in great distress. At age seventeen, she was four months pregnant and the condition was now noticed by all. The father was undetermined. In 1959 abortions were strictly illegal and even a hushed up subject, although she was now too far along for that even if available. She and the family were subject to ridicule and malicious gossip and the father's business was negatively affected. They decided to ask Florence to leave. She had no place to go and pleaded with Jen to take her in. With a spare room and the best of intentions they agreed to help and telegraphed her the money for a bus ticket.

Before the Thanksgiving holiday the whole town knew that the new teachers had a pregnant teenager living with them. Gossip was rampant and outlandish, even an asserted theory that Sid was the father and Jen encouraging infidelity. Small towns run the gamut from close friendships and maximum help to uncontrolled envy and spite. Parents united in complaining to the school about the immoral teachers and their possible corruption of the children.

The principal called them to her office and explained that she was being pressured to let them go. Instead of firing them, if they resigned she offered to get them the rest of the full year's salary and give them a letter of recommendation merely stating that they left for personal reasons. That way they could apply elsewhere for jobs.

Florence was very upset that she had caused such a turn of events. Jen assured her it was not her doing but just small minds directed towards evil ends. Under the weight of their crushed dreams, she cried extensively. For the first time ever she rejected Sid's attempts to comfort her. She balked at Sid's sentiment that things would eventually turn out for the good and their love would be stronger because of the set back. He did not know what else to say or do. Perhaps he was not convincing enough because he did not believe that himself. He felt a slight misgiving about who they were and what they were doing. All along there had been the confidence of knowing they were in total control of their destiny. Now, forces greater than themselves had made themselves known, and they were formidable enemies. It was the kind of reality that had to be accepted and reckoned with.

Having Florence there just added to the tension as there was a constant restraint on their actions and speech. Florence was pleasant enough and attempted to share tasks, but she was having a difficult pregnancy and it was taking its toll on her behavior. She needed plenty of bed rest, and Jen wound up waiting on her every need. They tried to be understanding of a young girl alone and afraid but with their own future now equally uncertain there was scant time for relaxation.

On New Year's Eve they greeted the start of a new decade with a certain trepidation. A special meal was capped with an optimistic toast at midnight. After going to bed, Jen wrapped her arms around him and spoke wistfully. "I wonder what the 60s will hold for us. I am sorry for any moment recently when I may have doubted you or us. I know our love is strong and will help us overcome any adversity. Yet, it is troubling knowing that an undefined future lays out there. Then, what will the 70s bring?"

Vain Regrets

It surely was a question to ponder. Sid took a pensive moment before speaking in a hushed tone, "That is a long way off. The present is mystery enough. I have a deep feeling that the next ten years will present major challenges for us and this nation. I dare say that there will be many children and adults who may need our guidance along the way. There will be causes that we cannot yet imagine that will need the full exertion of our hearts and minds to shed light on the darkness they bring. The one thing for sure is that we will be together to prepare and fight for the things we hold dear, and when we toast the arrival of 1970 it will be accompanied by one of our special kisses, hopefully on a bridge."

"And with our children at our side."

"If I was a fortune teller instead of a teacher that is what I would see clearly."

"Maybe we should just settle on the fortune part."

They kissed with renewed passion, a passion encompassing all that they were and all they were meant to be. "You are my treasure. Our love is our riches."

She responded in a sultry whisper, "I love you for any time and for all time."

NINE

The baby was born at the end of March, a girl they named Emily after collaborating on a name. Having a baby in the house quickly changed routines and outlook. Sid and Jen loved Emily as if she was their own, and that was not lost on Florence. She had been doing a great deal of thinking about her future as well as what to do with Emily. The ordeal had matured her. By May her mind was settled. She respected and admired the loving relationship between her sister and Sid, and in a way she was a bit envious. She loved the baby, but did not see her as part of her future. She proposed that Sid and Jen become Emily's parents, and that proposal was enthusiastically accepted and effectuated by a private adoption. The remainder of her plan was to join the newly established Peace Corps where basically young Americans were sent to developing nations to assist such nations in various ways. Still a minor, she needed and easily obtained parental consent just as she did to the adoption.

Jen stayed with the baby as Sid drove Florence to Washington to enlist in the Peace Corps. She was accepted immediately as the program was in its infancy and there was great eagerness to get as many recruits as possible. It was planned for her to go to Ethiopia to work in a health clinic. She was given temporary housing until all of the arrangements could be finalized.

While meeting with the Peace Corp. official, in conversation it came up that Sid and Jen were teachers. As long as he was here, the official suggested that Sid meet with a friend of his over at the National Park Service as the friend had mentioned there was a great need for teachers to become forest rangers as there was a growing emphasis for rangers to give guided tours of the national parks and the tours contained ever-increasing numbers of children. Sid made an appointment to meet with the friend the following day.

The friend eagerly greeted Sid, and he highlighted that a golden opportunity for a married teacher couple existed, and it would be acceptable if they had a child. A new ranger station was just about completed in the Bighorn National Recreation Area in Montana and there was an urgent need to get a park warden in place. It would a year-round resident position, and along with the usual park ranger functions including law enforcement and tours, from the station there would need to be constant monitoring of weather and observation for forest fires in the 120,000 acre park, as well operating the short wave radio unit. The spouse would also be a fully authorized ranger so that one of them could be at the station at all times, and thus an ideal situation for child care. The station was actually a multilevel house and fully furnished. It had a spectacular view, panoramic in nature, to enable seeing forest fires at great distances. A photograph was pulled from the file, and Sid's eyes lit up when he noticed there was even a foot bridge behind the house spanning a river with a picturesque waterfall. It was explained that the dire need arose because it had been difficult to get certain positions filled. It was made clear that the situation was one primarily of isolation and that the winters were long and brutal. That would not be acceptable to most people, but a loving and nature oriented couple could not be classified as most people.

Sid took the applications to be filled out and called Jen as soon as he got back to the hotel. Jen squealed with delight. Their time in the sun, rather their time in the park, was coming sooner than they dared to dream.

TEN

They were to move in to the park station on August 1. At least they would have part of the summer and the short autumn before the onset of the winter. There was much to take care of before the move.

Two weeks after sending in their measurements they received two summer and two winter uniforms each. To round out the clothing, they went to Hartford where there was a large Army and Navy store and bought all kinds of foul weather and winter gear, clothing and boots. A stop at two department stores and they had an array of baby and infant wear for any weather situation. The manuals for the short wave radio and the various weather instruments were studied and they felt confident they could work them. There would be two telephone lines to the station but it was indicated they would not be reliable.

Even though there would be an official jeep for use there, they figured it would be best to have two jeeps. They traded their car in for the ruggedest jeep available, and were able to get a good deal by paying all cash, most of which came from a quick lucrative sale of the lake lot.

Filling a U-Haul trailer pulled by the jeep, they headed west for what promised to be a new life and an adventure. The nearest town to the ranger station was thirty-seven miles away. They stopped there on the way to get initial groceries, mainly baby food and formula. The station was already stocked with emergency gear and supplies.

As soon as they unlocked the front door with the keys sent on in advance, they loved it all. Windows and decks looked out for what seemed to be endless miles of a majestic landscape which would warm the heart of any naturalist. Dishes, pots, and every conceivable utensil could be found in the spacious kitchen. A year's supply of linens and towels lined closets. Four industrial washers and driers were housed in a utility room also lined with shelves containing enough equipment to fortify a small army. A dozen telescopes and binoculars were laid out on a work table.

It was exciting getting acquainted with the house, its layout, and contents. The master bedroom was large enough to also hold Emily's crib until she was old enough to be moved in to one of the other close by bedrooms. It appeared nothing was overlooked in sustaining the occupants safety and comfort. Jen's astute observation said it all. "So, this is what Heaven must be like."

Electricity ran to the station although it had a propane generator as a back up system. The building was heated by a Yukon system run by wood with propane kicking in if the temperature fell below a certain mark. Four massive propane tanks were buried behind the station. Wood was stacked beneath the decks.

The garage under the station proper was large enough to house the two jeeps as well as the small tour bus. Just beyond the garage was the station's own gasoline pump with a buried storage tank. They were told that the propane tanks and the gasoline tank would be topped off before the rigor of winter set in.

The entire ground floor was for the public. There were restrooms, vending machines, a first aid vestibule, and an exhibit area that they would eventually set up. In season when the station was open to the public, a designated crew came in regularly to clean the restrooms and other public areas, and a vending company tended to the machines.

In the darkness of the first night, they went out to the bridge and under a full canopy of stars and the crescendo of the river and waterfall they held each other close. With a special kiss they acknowledged that their love and a touch of luck brought them to this wonderful place. It represented a happiness to savor. There was a slight remorse that the Connecticut situation fell apart. The teaching had been stimulating and the plan for the lake house was worth looking forward to. However, it all paled compared to this captivating place and the promise of emotional and physical rewards attached to its operation. All of their talents and creativity would be called upon, and they eagerly embraced the challenge.

The next day, the three seasonal park rangers who lived beyond the park came to the station to meet them. Their main function was to patrol the camping sites which were open from Memorial Day to Labor Day.

The official opening and operation of the station was two weeks off, and they took full advantage that one of them had to be at the station at all times until then. Each day they took the tour bus out to familiarize themselves with its operation and the roads through the park. They took copious notes on the vegetation, rock formations, scenic overlooks, and animal life. The ride was often bumpy, but Emily usually slept through it all. The park was a magical place and it beckoned to them. Without doubt this was their special calling and entrenched future. They would be living a dream that a short time ago they had no idea they could dream.

ELEVEN

They had picked up an interesting assortment of items from the woods, overlooks, and trails so that the exhibit area was not completely barren by opening day. Over the winter they would make a complete exhibit arrangement that could be changed in whole or in part as the need arose.

There was a mimeograph machine at the station and reams of paper. They ran off a bunch of temporary leaf albums that could be distributed to children. During the winter they would compose a detailed information booklet with information on the park and its vegetation and animals, and would include a map of trails and roads. A leaf album would be incorporated in that booklet along with questions to stimulate keener observations.

Opening day was on a Saturday so a fair number of people showed up. Most were campers or weekend hikers, and Sid and Jen greeted them warmly. They successfully fielded all questions and threw out ideas to get the folks to explore parts of the park. The waterfall behind the station was a popular draw, and many people would go out on the bridge to admire it and take pictures.

Sid took a few groups out on tour, and that went well. Visitors and tours would become an enjoyable routine, and they looked forward to interaction with the children on the tours and at the station. After all, the park was in effect a wondrous schoolhouse filled with sights and sounds to learn about and remember. A respect and admiration for nature developed in the young would undoubtedly stay with them their entire lives.

Observing the weather proved fascinating. A panoramic view of cloud formations, often appearing close enough that all it seemed they would have to do would be to reach up to touch them, was an ongoing magical display. Actual weather systems on the move could be watched, and it was engrossing to see bands of rain track across the park. Rainbows, often with vivid colors, were not uncommon. Jen took particular delight in the first double rainbow that developed. She spouted part of a rhyme that she had committed to memory as a young girl:

> *I washed my hopes to brightness*
> *and then hung them up to dry*
> *Over a gleaming rainbow*
> *far-flung across the sky.*

As a carryover from their romantic past and the desire to perpetuate a meaningful act, unless the weather was nasty each morning and evening they would walk out to the bridge for a warm embrace and a special kiss. A life without love seemed so distant, and they remarked often that they pitied those who live a loveless life.

The river and waterfall were additional enchanting features. The rushing water was a soothing sound in the otherwise vast solitude. With it running beneath them when on the bridge and cascading down the waterfall, for them it represented a strong and perpetual underpinning of their love.

Memorial Day came and went, and the camping sites were closed. They had the most frequent contact with Frank Hankershaw, one of the seasonal rangers who lived closest to the park area. His wife, Ann, came over to visit often and since she loved to bake she would usually bring some creation that was very much appreciated since Jen rarely baked. They had no children and Ann enjoyed playing with Emily. She offered to watch her as Frank took care of the station if Sid and Jen ever had to go somewhere together. That was fortuitous because they had to take Emily to the pediatrician a couple of times and Jen had to check in with a doctor as she was two months pregnant.

Whenever they were in town, they would pick up the station mail at the post office. A letter had come from Florence detailing her activities and reactions at the health clinic in Ethiopia. She had also met and fallen in love with an American theology student who was doing a stint with the Peace Corps, and they planned to marry after they got back to the United States and he finished his studies and found a church to pastor at. She had not told him about Emily and had decided there was no need to do so. Once again she expressed her gratitude for what Sid and Jen had done for her, and she was at peace knowing that Emily was so loved.

The autumn was spectacular with classic tree colors. It was short-lived, however, as the first frost set in early and fierce winter winds took hold. The first significant snow fell early in November, and that brought forth a new scenic wonderland.

As forewarned, the winter was long. Yet, in its own way it was pleasurable. They had ample time to work on the projects they had been planning for, and they also decided to coauthor a book on the joy of learning about nature. Emily started walking and cooing, and there was the added excitement of the forthcoming baby. If one had to be confined it is best if it is with the one who is loved. That has its own rewards and fulfillment. There is also the added contentment that the quiet moments foster.

TWELVE

A welcomed late spring brought a panorama of flowering bushes and trees. Does scampered with their mothers in the woods. New discoveries of nature's wonderful diversity were made daily, and for those who appreciated all of the unfolding it truly was remarkable. The outside world might be staggering through difficult and trying times, but there was true order and sense in this place.

In June, Bennett Allen was born. They called him Ben from the start. Emily, who was just beginning to talk, called the baby Benjy. Ann came over every day for the first two weeks after the baby was home. She was of great help and was delighted to do it, and Emily was coaxed to call her Aunt Ann.

The addition of the new child raised the loving activity level of the home. To fulfill their earlier expressed desire to have a dog in the home, they adopted a brother and sister mixed breed at the shelter in town. That proved a fulfilling element as they had imagined. For all of the ensuing years, dogs scampered through the house. They never had less than two and, at one time, they had five. It was sad when they passed on, but there was always the comforting feature of knowing they gave them a good life and a loving home. People with loving hearts love animals as well as other people.

Until one has loved an animal, a part of
one's soul remains unawakened.

— Anatole France

The arrival of the baby completed a reconciliation with the families. Both sets of grandparents came for a visit. Sid's parents were swept up in the children, and his father was duly impressed by the station and Sid's great responsibility. He even mentioned when they were leaving that he was very proud of the way he turned out. Any earlier misgivings and negative thoughts about Jen were overshadowed by the now capable image of her as a wife, mother, and ranger.

At first, Jen's parents were reluctant to react closely with Emily as they knew she was really Florence's child. All of that dissipated when they became enchanted by her delightful toddler antics and how beautiful baby Ben was. Having many children of their own made it easy to relate to a growing family. In a conversation they had in private one evening, Jen's mother confessed that she had been quite worried when Jen was young about what would become of her because she was so unsure of herself. She apologized if she in any way was the cause of any of her weaknesses or failures. She boasted about what a fine woman and mother Jen had become. Jen easily forgave her because a life of love had made her strong, confident, and capable. An expanded heart and a forgiving tendency were residuals. The parents also mentioned to her as an aside that Sid was, in the final analysis, a good man for her.

Josh and Ally also stopped for a brief visit on a cross-country trip they were taking during Josh's summer vacation. They had married in January and well understood why Sid and Jen were unable to attend the wedding. They sure did appreciate the large monetary wedding gift sent on to them. The visit was pleasant, and Ally proved to be as angelic as Josh had described.

Deana did not visit but would call from time to time. She was teaching in Boston and was finding it challenging. She had made numerous friends and dated often. That one special man had not yet entered her life but she was not without hope. Another Sid had to be out there somewhere. She sent a beautiful outfit for the baby along with a warm note of friendship.

The first full summer at the station was a beehive of activity. The popularity of the Park with its numerous recreational inducements brought many visitors. Tours were a constant and all sorts of people problems prompted attention. Being so busy the days flew by, and the quiet family times in the evenings revived them. Through trial and error they devised shortcuts to handle and predict certain situations. The weekly reports filed to Washington were packed with accomplishments. The numerous suggestions offered for improvements were considered and many implemented. All of this made them feel good about what they were doing. They had read and heard about people answering their calling. Both had the firm conviction that this is what they were meant to be and to do.

THIRTEEN

Two years later Dorey Park was born and became the newest animated addition to the Corwin family. Rachael Bell followed fifteen months later. Love certainly had room for more children but the space in the station did not so they proclaimed the family unit complete.

With two teachers as the parents, the children were home schooled. It was also impractical to have them go to the public schools which were a long distance from the station and they would have had to drive them when much of the winter it was impossible to drive anywhere.

All of the growing years for the children were spent in the Park, and the communion with nature was omnipresent. It was ingrained in their being. They played and worked in and around every inch of the terrain, and there were probably few plants and trees that they had not touched. The animals were not afraid of them, and they were conversant with their mannerisms and instincts. The dogs in the home were a carryover from the animals in the wild, and the dogs would usually accompany them in the ever-widening explorations. As they aged, the children helped with the station and visitor activities and it made the entire operation run more efficiently. Over the years the station became more and more computerized, and this enabled the children to adapt to an advancing technological society.

All of the children went to the State University. Each had a partial academic scholarship and with the reduced tuition for instate residents, it was not a great financial strain. Throughout the college years holidays and the summers took on particular meaning because the family was then intact. Jovial times would occur wherever they gathered, whether it was around the dining room table or in the great room and they would remember and relate happenings from life in their unusual habitat. Instances which may have been serious when they happened would take on a humorous bent in the retelling, such as when Dorey discovered poison ivy and Rachael learned that it is often easier to climb up a tree than to climb down it.

As the children made their own pathways through life, Sid and Jen were revered parents and role models. They were consulted often and shared in meaningful events. Travel to weddings, births, and monumental achievements became memorable excursions. Emily had become Director of one of the historic plantations in Charleston, South Carolina. She married a journalist and they had two children. Rachael worked as her deputy assistant at the plantation and was married to a high school teacher. They had one child. The two families lived three miles apart. Dorey was a landscape architect specializing in older gardens also in Charleston. Her spouse was a nursery owner she had met in her work environment and they often did projects together. They had three children. Ben had become a park ranger and actually replaced Sid as the Park Warden while Sid and Jen continued on as park rangers under him. He had never married declaring he had yet to meet a woman as conversant with nature as his family members and who could withstand the trial of harsh winters in isolation. Having him in place there freed up the parents to sojourn to other sites.

When one leads a contented life, it is often difficult to keep track of time. It was now 2009, and in many ways for Sid and Jen it was that proverbial grain of sand on the beach of time. It could have been the month before that they were at the college kissing on the bridge. It could have been last week that they moved with Emily to the Park. It could have been just yesterday that the other children were born. Each day, month, and year had been a blessing. Life had been full and happy. A few illnesses and injuries did not sidetrack them. They had raised serious and productive children and had taught them to live and fight for causes they believed in. There had been many examples they had set for them, including the Civil Rights Movement, the anti-Vietnam War crusade, environmental threats including global warming, and opposition to political leaders who had bad ideas for the nation and its people. The specter of nuclear annihilation still hung over them.

This year marked two special occasions. It would be their fiftieth wedding anniversary and it would be fifty years that they were park rangers. The retirement papers had already been submitted, and they would be financially stable receiving two federal pensions. The children were planning a gala anniversary celebration in Charleston with all of the children, grandchildren, and Jen's siblings to attend. Florence had tragically died in 1961 in Ethiopia from dysentery, her dreams gone in the process. Their parents had died earlier at various times.

As much as they loved the Park and the station home, it was time to move on. Before facing the rigors of another winter they would move to Charleston with its temperate climate and where three of the four children were settled. Emily had found for them a quaint cottage in a newly built active adult retirement community with its own ponds and nature trails. It was aptly called The Bridges as each cottage in the community had its own bridge that had to be crossed to reach the residence. Naturally, the children watching over the years and with hundreds of stories knew the significance of a bridge to the old folks.

It was going to be a new adventure and they were looking forward to it. Before they left the station and saying good-bye to Ben until they saw him at the celebration in Charleston, they went out to the footbridge. The bridge was the fourth replacement since their initial arrival. Fifty years of accumulated embraces and kisses. It still had that special meaning symbolizing their love and togetherness. A love that was their lifeline from a lonely and lost childhood, through an unsettling teenage period, and leading them to a maturity where the seeds of that love brought bountiful harvests. The kiss was as fresh as the very first one on the bridge at the college. It was the repeated confirmation that they were and would be alive and emotionally vibrant to the end.

EPILOGUE

In His World was finished. It was not great literature, but Roger knew Sid would have enjoyed it. He could almost hear him exclaim, "That's the character I wanted to be! That's the kind of woman I needed! That's the love and life I should have had!"

Roger's loyal following will probably find it interesting, and the same comments from them after each publication will probably be forthcoming that it is an unusual story and they do not know how he does it but it is totally different from all of the other books. Placing regrets in proper perspective was still his main goal. He hoped that point came across forcefully. It was also meaningful to him that the poignant dream of an old man who professed to have had an empty life inspired the book. Sid's final days were the realization of the significance of the turning point.

The day after the book was published, Roger was driving in an area he had not been to before. He noticed a little park, and since it was such a beautiful day he pulled into the empty parking area and strolled down a path. Writing about the allure of nature in the book made him cognizant of the trees and flowers. Spring certainly was such a delightful time of the year. Everything was fresh and new, as if all could be reborn and revitalized. There was a sweet fragrance in the air, and song birds were nearby.

He rounded a bend in the trail and stopped in his tracks. Before him was an old wooden footbridge spanning a stream. He lingered on the bridge. The sensation came over him that he was in Sid's and Jen's world. If only all of humanity could feel that love!

VAIN REGRETS

POSTSCRIPT

The bittersweet tears shed over graves
are for words left unsaid and deeds undone.

— Harriet Beecher Stowe

ONE

There were two more novels published after *In His Way*. Then, Roger Kimbel, who usually had his protagonist face up to and adjust to reality, could not avoid his own confrontation. While his physical condition was good for a man in his eighties, the continuing power of his mind was waning. The medical condition was diagnosed as dementia and an approach to a moderate form of Alzheimer's. He did not care what term or label was given to it, it was upsetting and scary to have gaps in his thinking and memory. Losing control of the direction and clarity of thoughts is devastating to an author. The medicine tried was of no help and actually made it worse because added to the situation were periods when he was in a stupor. As hard on him as it was, it was even more problematic for his wife, Jean. She was at a loss in what to do or say to alleviate the emotional and mental anguish.

Interestingly, and no one was able to adequately explain to him why such was the case, his dreams reflected the awake form of disability, and he forgot more than he remembered about them. He very well might have dreamed away finally the regrets about Regina Stern or the fearful inaction relating to the trip South to assist in black voter registration. If he could not remember that, then it was no use whatsoever and any semblance to his world was lost. He wished Sid was still around so that they could discuss all of the ramifications.

Speaking of Sid, he had not met anyone like him who apparently could relive a life in dreams. That made him especially honored to have captured those dreams in the book. Sure, he had met and tried to help a bunch of seniors who had vain regrets, but it was not the same. Even among that group, he no longer could remember them all.

One he could recall quite clearly, although he was not sure how long ago it happened, was with Leslie Cantor. He probably remembered it because a regret she had in some ways was similar to the regret he had about Regina.

Leslie was in a nursing home when he met her. It so happened that the home was giving her a party to celebrate her ninetieth birthday when he had delivered a signed copy of one of his books to the Director of the home who had bought it upon the recommendation of a friend. As long as he was there, he was invited to the party.

After the festivities were over, he stayed to talk to Leslie. She seemed to be an interesting lady, still sharp in wit and wisdom, and she expressed a desire to chat with him. The party goers gradually disbursed and he and Leslie were the only ones left in the party room. Leslie told him to pull a chair over close to the wheelchair she was in. Her voice was strong considering her age and that she had talked so much during the party. "It's been a long time since a man has looked at me with admiring eyes."

He smiled and patted her lean arm. "They are fools and do not know what they are missing."

After he told her who he was and why he was there, she asked him to tell her about his books. She explained that her eyes were too poor to read anymore but she was interested to know what went through his mind while he was writing. He had to reflect on that for a moment himself. "As the story teller, I am the mover of the events and take the substance of the characters I am manipulating. There are thoughts, emotions, and events playing upon each other. I am the captain at the wheel of the ship, and winds varying from strong to weak fill the sails."

Thin parched lips parted in the hint of a knowing smile. "And what is your favorite book about?"

After detailing *In His World*, she looked directly into his eyes. "Is it too late for me to relive a regret?"

"Do you dream?"

"Yes, powerful dreams at times."

"Then you can do it. Sid did it."

"Too bad Sid and I never met. I have one monumental regret in my life." Her gaze shifted to the window and he wished he could see what she was looking for.

"Do you want to talk about it?"

"You won't think much of me when I tell you."

"I don't judge others because I don't want them to judge me. I am already fully impressed by and with you, and I doubt if anything could shake that. One thing us older folk know is that we just need to accept who we are as it is a waste of time and energy to do otherwise."

Again, she looked off in the distance, and he was not sure she was going to speak any more. Her look shifted to him. "I had a successful life as a fashion designer. I was just twenty when I graduated from Design and Fashion School, and luckily landed an apprentice job with a leading designer. I was swept up in it, but secretly what I wanted more than anything else was to have a husband and children. A young man, a photographer trying to break into the fashion business, kept following me around taking my picture all of the time. He claimed I was very photogenic and beautiful. He had no money really and not good at conversation. In fact, I thought he was dull and boring. I was intent on the party life around me and the excitement of a fast moving job. He declared he was in love with me and asked me to marry him. I turned him down, sure that many interesting and wealthy men would be after me. He disappeared and never came back. Yes, there were many men but not a single marriage proposal. No husband and no children. Instead of motherhood I wound up in spinsterhood. If I had to do it all over again, I would have married my photographer, and now my children would be regular visitors here. I get no visitors because I have no one who cares about me, no one who loves me." She looked off again and spoke in a near whisper. "Success is an elusive factor in life. It brings satisfaction but no true happiness. Roger, and I hope you don't mind me calling you Roger, facing death alone is not what I ever wanted."

He grasped her hand. The fingers were cold, and the skin was brittle. "Dear heart, I have a similar regret in my life. I was very mean and hurtful to a young woman who idolized me. While I found love eventually, to this day I realize I may have lost more than I ever gained. Maybe, like Sid, you can relive your life in a dream, and as long as you are still alive you have an opportunity each day to do something for yourself or others to make the day more meaningful. Do not fault yourself for anything in your past. What you did at the time may not appear right in hindsight, but you did what you determined was best for yourself at the time even if it did not work out that way. Being human means we make mistakes, and sometimes they are large and serious mistakes. How about I come over whenever I can and I will read to you from my books?"

A sly smile came to the pinched lips, and a baby tear rolled down a ninety year old cheek. "I would like that. I would like that very much."

TWO

Over the next fourteen months Roger visited Leslie frequently. He would help her out of the wheelchair so she could sit in one of the upholstered arm chairs in the sun room. They would hug, laugh, and chatter without restriction as to content. He would read aloud from his books as she put her head back and closed her eyes. Just when he would think she had fallen asleep and he would stop reading, she would urge him to continue or ask him a question or make a comment about what he had just read.

The nursing home telephoned him to advise him that Leslie had a stroke the night before and was in the hospital. By the time he arrived there she was unconscious and close to death. He would never know whether she knew he was with her when she died. He kissed a cold cheek when he left the bedside. At least he was comforted by the fact that she was not alone at the end. Leslie was one grand lady and would have been a wonderful mother.

He made other friends at the nursing home during that time. Leslie had told others of his warm and receptive conversation and caring. Some had just overheard the sessions the two held. Roger wished he could remember them all and their stories, but besides recollections fading in and out, he was wrestling with what he found to be a more trying situation, the mental dilemma of what was real and what he might just be imagining. He started questioning himself. Did this really happen? Was it a scene or character from one of his books? Was it a person he knew or he thought he knew or wanted to know?

For some reason, and he would be hard pressed to say why, one particular nursing home resident and her story stuck with him. Sally Hauck was another ninety year old, and she had been there for over twenty years, ever since her husband died and her one daughter would not care for her in her home. Sally had been a high school music teacher and played the viola. Her husband had been a drug representative for a large pharmaceutical company and had traveled frequently.

One dreary rainy day, Roger had just spent an hour with Leslie and she had been transported back to her room. He had lingered in the sun room which was fairly dark because of the weather. Usually it was bright and cheery. He was in a pensive mood as an aftermath of Leslie's probing mind. He was looking out of the window watching the wind bend the branches and leaves as if a giant hand had caressed them. Out of the corner of his eye he caught a glimpse of a woman sitting in a chair in the shadows of the room. He approached her. "Hello there. Can I help you?"

It was not so dark that he could not observe she was quite elderly with short thin hair and glasses that had slipped part way down a long nose. It was a moment before she answered. Her voice was raspy and quivered slightly but there was no doubt it was cultured. "You already have."

"I am glad about that."

"I have listened to you reading at times, and there is a form of music in your words."

He chuckled. "I haven't been accused of that before."

"I was a musician. Songs in your heart are reflected in your words."

"If you were a musician, you still are."

"True. I should have said I am a musician. I can no longer play music but it remains in my soul. Roger, I believe, I am Sally."

"Nice to meet you, Sally."

"Leslie has told me you are easy to talk to."

"I believe Leslie is an angel in a people's disguise."

"You are now meeting the Devil."

"I doubt that."

"Believe it. If you have a moment to listen, I would like to tell you something I have never told any one else before. I need to tell someone before I die. There should be no secrets in the grave."

He pulled up a chair and sat directly in front of her. "I have time. As a writer, I try to be a good listener."

She closed her eyes and moistened her lips with the tip of her tongue. The glasses slipped a bit further down her nose. Her eyes remained closed the entire time she spoke, perhaps trying to see what she was describing so she would get it right. "People do not know and do not appreciate how lonely it can be in a nursing home. Yes, there are people here and they are all around, and things are going on, but loneliness is a personal thing. In the many quiet moments when your thoughts are your only company, loneliness can be overwhelming."

If he would have known then what he knew now, he would have been able to interject that he was experiencing a far greater loneliness because even his thoughts were abandoning him. So, he could relate to how she feels.

There was a glass of water on the table besides her chair. Slowly, she picked it up and drank from it, putting it down carefully. Her eyes were closed the entire time. "I was lonely long before I came here. I had an unsatisfying marriage, and my daughter was a social butterfly and rarely at home. My husband was gone for long stretches of time and even when he was home we had little to talk about. He was far afield from my world of music, and he was indifferent about me. Why we married in the first place is a life long mystery. To fill up my time, I taught music at the high school and joined a string quartet that played and practiced in the evenings. To make a long story short for an old woman, and as shocking as it going to sound, I had a long and torrid affair with Jack who played the violin. We shared a love of music, and life for that time was good. I did not feel lonely and did not even think in terms of being distant from the world. He was married as well but could not bring himself to leave his wife. Eventually, the affair ended. I could not bear being close to him so I quit the quartet. My husband did not know, and my daughter knew and hated me for it and has been hostile all of these years. Loneliness set in again, and only lonely people realize the negative power it commands." Her eyes opened. "I became the Devil."

He knew he had to measure his words carefully. "That does not make you the Devil or even devilish. Seeking love and understanding is not a sign of depravity but merely reflects a human need. That you found it for however long is an accomplishment and not a negative. We all seek to fill the voids in our lives. Hopefully, the memory of what you had gives you more comfort than anguish. I hope your telling me acts as a release and quiets your restless doubts. Also, sharing your thoughts with me should make you less lonely. I do not think badly of you. In fact, I admire your facing your conscience and your past. Do not let it haunt you as a regret. You reached out for what was lacking in your life. Life is just too short not to grab every happiness when you can."

"Thank you. I feel better right now because of what you said and because it is not bottled up inside of me. I do not know how I will feel later."

"Let's talk about it after the next time I see Leslie."

"Alright."

THREE

It was obvious that the scheme was concocted to help him. Even in his deteriorating condition, Roger figured the downward spiral was accelerating because there was so much concern surrounding him. Visits to and from the children and grandchildren were more frequent, and everyone was paying extra attention to him. That was all fine with him. He loved his children and grandchildren greatly.

While he could concentrate, instead of writing he devoted the time to organizing his papers and affairs. He had already discussed with Jean what to do about his books and other writings, but while he was able he wrote out a detailed plan for her to follow after he was gone. This carried over for inclusion of all of their joint financial affairs.

Speaking about being gone, his new determination was to be gone on his own terms. This was his secret choice, and he did not want it to ripen to a regret if it did not happen. Actually, the idea came to him by way of Neil Coventry. The idea was clear, but Neil was not. Roger thought he was a man that Sally introduced to him at the home and with whom he had a series of conversations. Then, again, he might have been a character he was creating in his mind for a future book. Not that it mattered at this point. It was a reasonable idea whether it was his or Neil's.

Neil's story was not an easy one to relate because of the various complexities and actors. When he was in his forties, his mother had been hospitalized with an advanced stage of stomach cancer. She had in the early days been a wonderful mother and exemplary wife. Over the years a gradual transformation brought her to a different posture. She was cantankerous and emotionally difficult. Nothing her husband or Neil tried to do for her was recognized or appreciated. Rather, she was tyrannical and uncompromising, and she found fault in everything. He was an adult and not living at home so it did not have as much of an impact on him as it did on his father who was being sapped of his sanity. At the hospital, his father pleaded with him to help him to be set free so that he could enjoy some final years in peace. Neil knew exactly what he meant. He had a candid talk with the doctor in charge of the treatment, and he was more understanding than Neil had expected. Probably, that was because his mother was terminal and it just meant hastening the process. She was being given morphine for pain, and the administration of a bit more brought on death. Seeing his mother in those final moments brought on mixed emotions. He had done it for his father, but it always lurked in the background of his own being whether he had done the right thing.

Roger was faced with making two decisions. How to effectuate a death wish? What to do in the meantime? Some might say he was morbid, and maybe even selfish not to basically consider the wishes of his loved ones, but he was convinced that it should be his decision and he had to be sure the timing and circumstances were right.

He was not prepared to write another book. It would be frustrating to start one and not finish it. He could, however, still discuss his philosophy with those who might benefit from it. If they could afford it, Roger might have tried to talk Jean into putting him in a nursing home, although she was adamant about caring for him. He was unable to drive himself, so he had her drive him to the home once a week for the day so that he could mingle with the residents. The administrators knew him well by this time and knew his intentions were good and the plan was agreed to. They even brought him lunch.

Residents would come and go, and he already knew some of them. He would spend the day in the sun room where it was warm and restful, and a haven without going outside. He would talk to any that cared to chat. As with Sally and Neil, just telling somebody about a regret harbored within served as a release. Perhaps, it was even a form of seeking forgiveness.

Morgan Faitherly had been an auctioneer in a rural county in Pennsylvania. In that business there are ample opportunities to take advantage of people and situations. In the early years, Morgan was as honest and forthright as he could be. Gradually, greed and temptation led

Vain Regrets

him down a different path. In certain situations it was easy to get away with not paying people what they deserved to get. Widows, who knew nothing about the value of their husband's collections, and who may have been eager to get rid of them because they were large and unsightly, or they reminded them of the deceased, or they may have been embarrassed by them, such as toys, it was easy to offer them to buy the collection for what Morgan knew was a small fraction of the actual value. If that method did not work, he would actually put it up at auction and a shill would buy it on his behalf with a low winning bid if it was not lost to a higher bid. That way, he wound up with the collection and also deducted the auctioneer's commission from the proceeds. Another easy prey were those persons, usually elderly ones who were moving and downsizing. If the sale of the house presented time and logistical problems, such people might turn over a whole bunch of items to be auctioned off on their behalf. He would put them up for auction after the folks had moved away and he could juggle the accounting any way he wanted to. He could just ignore the whole transaction knowing the people would have too much difficulty doing anything about it, or he might claim lower amounts were tended. Morgan realized in these later years that he had hurt many people, people who most likely needed the money they deserved more than he did. He would do it differently if he could turn the clock back.

FOUR

On one of the visits to the home, Roger cut his finger on the tip of a nail that was protruding from the back of the chair he was sitting in. It did not appear to be a bad cut, but the bleeding continued. A staffer suggested he go down to see the resident nurse.

Wanda Atwater had been the nurse at the home for twelve years. She was a registered nurse, and after a stint at a hospital a realization that she had a special empathy for older folks led her to apply for this job when it came open. The nexus with seniors undoubtedly came from her being raised by her grandparents, two warm and caring people who gave her a loving and secure foundation for life's exploits.

Wanda was doing paperwork at her desk when Roger knocked on the office door. "Come in." She looked up as Roger entered and saw the tissue wrapped around the finger.

He looked upon a woman he guessed to be in her forties, slightly overweight, and with soft features. A woman in a white uniform exudes a pristine and motherly nature. "Sorry to bother you. I am a visitor and had a small accident."

"Come in and let's go into the examining room and I'll take a look at it."

"I am Roger Kimbel."

"I know who you are. I have seen you around here many times over the years, and many of my friends have talked about you."

He could not resist asking, "Kind talk, I hope?"

"Yes, almost saintly. I am Nurse Wanda."

She examined the finger, cleaned it with peroxide and put a small piece of gauze over the cut and secured it with tape. "Good as new."

"Good as old. Thank you."

Her touch had been soft and comforting. "Perhaps, you can put me in your next book."

"There will be no more books." He proceeded to elaborate on his medical condition.

She reached out and held his hand, careful not to dislodge the bandage. "You seem to have accepted it well. I see such disappointing features far too often, and it certainly does help to face it straight on with resolve. Maybe, we should go out on a date while you still know you have to pay for me."

He laughed at her humor, putting him further at ease. He sure did like this nurse! "My wife will insist on being a chaperone."

"So be it. You seem to be enough of a man that two women will be to your liking."

He laughed again. "So be it."

She did not let go of his hand. He sensed he had just made the right kind of friend to help him with his desired end. "After the date, you can do me a tremendous favor."

Her smile was warm, and she tightened the hold on his hand. "I know what you have in mind. I can and I will. Over the years, I have helped those who have asked it of me. I believe in death with dignity. Mercy killing is highly controversial, but I have never had a problem with it. I think it is the most humane act I can do. I don't look at it as helping people to die. I help them make a wish come true."

He traced his thought processes that had brought him to this point. All the while she continued to hold his hand, and he stared at what he could only describe as the face of an angel.

Each time that Roger came to the home he dropped in to see Wanda. Every visit was reassuring. He hoped he had been half as understanding through his life as she was.

Two months later Roger decided the time had arrived. Lucidity was diminishing and he was having great difficulty focusing his mind in desired directions. His determination was unshakeable.

Wanda gave him a large capsule to be taken when he went to bed. He would drift away during the night. There would be no tell-tale signs, no residue in the unlikely event there was an autopsy. Death would appear natural.

He gave Wanda a final hug. "Thank you for believing in me and helping me."

"You are my kind of man, Roger."

"And, you are definitely my kind of woman."

That night he took the capsule. He climbed into bed and draped his arm over Jean's sleeping body that was turned away from him. He was at peace with himself and with the world.

The last thing he was aware of was clearly seeing the image of Regina Stern. She was smiling and holding a bouquet of flowers. She reached her arm out towards him. He grabbed hold of her hand tightly, realizing that it was actually Wanda's hand.

When Jean awoke in the morning, she knew right away by the cold stiff arm around her what had happened. She lay still as the tears welled up in her eyes and cascaded down along her face. She did not know how long she laid there, but when she did get up she saw the note on the bed stand.

My Darling Jean —

*I love you deeply and that love, especially your
love for me, inspired me and allowed me to
fulfill my passion for writing and to help
others with their regrets in life. I have not
a single regret about our years of togetherness.
Rather, I celebrate every minute.*

*Please hug and kiss the children and
grandchildren and tell them that I
love them all and am proud of them.
I wish them happy and full lives.
Their mother/grandmother will see
to that I am sure.*

I embrace you eternally.

Remember me as I used to be.

I sign the final chapter of my life,
a full and contented life.

— **Roger Kimbel**

www.ingramcontent.com/pod-product-compliance
Lightning Source LLC
Chambersburg PA
CBHW031844170626
46807CB00004B/1622